A Forever Friend

Read all of

MARGUERITE HENRY'S Misty Inn

books!

#1 Welcome Home!

#2 Buttercup Mystery

#3 Runaway Pony

#4 Finding Luck

And coming soon:

#6 Pony Swim

MARGUERITE HENRY'S Misty Inn

A Forever Friend

By Judy Katschke

Illustrated by Serena Geddes

ALADDIN

New York London Toronto Sydney New Delhi

ALADDIN
An imprint of Simon & Schuster Children's Publishing Division
1230 Avenue of the Americas, New York, NY 10020
First Aladdin paperback edition October 2016

Also available in an Aladdin hardcover edition.

Book designed by Laura Lyn DiSiena
The text of this book was set in Century Expanded.
Manufactured in the United States of America 1216 OFF
10 9 8 7 6 5 4 3 2
Library of Congress Control Number 2016936155
ISBN 978-1-4814-6986-9 (hc)
ISBN 978-1-4814-6985-2 (pbk)
ISBN 978-1-4814-6987-6 (eBook)

For Caryn

Chapter 1

"HOW DOES DEEP-DISH PIZZA SOUND?" DAD teased. "Or Chicago-style hot dogs dripping with relish, tomatoes, and onions?"

Willa Dunlap's mouth watered buckets. Those were some of the yummiest foods they ate when they lived in Chicago. But they weren't in Chicago anymore.

"How about cinnamon buns?" Dad tried again.

"I love cinnamon buns!" Willa exclaimed, then shook her head and said, "Nope, nope . . . and nope."

It was still breakfast time at Misty Inn's Family Farm Restaurant, but never too early for Willa's dad to brainstorm his next meal.

"I don't understand, Willa," Dad said, pulling a pan of cranberry muffins from the oven. "Your best friend from Chicago is visiting for five days. Don't you want some Chicago dishes to make her feel at home?"

Willa gave it a thought.

She remembered the first day she, her parents, and her younger brother, Ben, had arrived at Chincoteague Island. They were greeted by the salty fresh air, an old Victorian house, and a huge pan of fried oysters, courtesy of a new friend and neighbor.

Just one crunch into the crispy golden delight made Willa almost forget about deep-dish pizza—even cinnamon buns.

"Chicago food is awesome, Dad," Willa agreed. "But if Kate is going to live with us for almost a week, I want her to experience everything Chincoteague. That means seafood."

"Someone say seafood?" Ben asked.

Willa hadn't noticed Ben standing behind her. Her little brother was hungrily munching on a warm muffin.

"Or," Ben said, before opening his mouth to show his crumby tongue, "see food."

"Yuck," Willa complained. "That's gross, Ben."

"What's gross?" Mom asked as she walked into the kitchen from her home office. "Ben, did

you roll your eyelids inside out again?"

Ben quickly shut his mouth and shook his head.

Willa was glad her little brother had started to come out of his shell since moving to Chincoteague. But what if he flashed his crumby tongue while Kate was there?

"Willa, did you finish your chores?" Mom asked. "They need to be done before Kate and her parents get here."

Willa nodded yes and then pulled her latest

list from the pocket of her shorts: "Things to Do Before Kate Gets Here." She loved lists. She also loved checking off each chore, like:

1. Make Kate's bed.
2. Hang welcome sign on door.
3. Clear out two drawers for Kate's clothes.
4. Clean the barn and groom the ponies.

Willa liked the last chore best. Even though taking care of her pony, Starbuck, and their boarder pony, Buttercup, wasn't really a chore. To Willa it was fun.

"I'm sorry Kate's parents can't stay at Misty Inn," Mom told Willa. "But it's the first week of summer and all the rooms were booked before you and Kate made plans."

"It's okay, Mom." Willa smiled. "With Kate staying in my room, we'll get to spend more time together."

"I still can't believe it," Dad said, shaking his head. "We just opened Misty Inn for business in the spring. Who ever thought we'd be totally booked by summer?"

Willa couldn't believe it either. But turning the house into a bed-and-breakfast had been her parents' plan. Dad would be head chef. Mom would be "head honcho" of Misty Inn, as she liked to call herself sometimes.

It didn't take long for Willa to make great new friends on Chincoteague Island, where her mom had grown up. New friends were awesome, but Willa knew there was nothing like an old friend. And that was Kate.

Where was Kate already? "Weren't Kate and parents supposed to be here last night?" she asked.

"It's a long drive from Chicago," Mom reminded a lot more patiently. "Mrs. Worthington e-mailed that they wanted to stop and do some sightseeing along the way."

Stop? Willa did not like the sound of that.

"What if Kate's parents forgot to set an alarm clock at their hotel?" Willa asked. "What if they're so busy sightseeing they forget to visit me?"

"What if you go upstairs and make sure your room is extra tidy for Kate?" Dad asked with a smile. "That ought to keep you busy until she gets here."

Willa looked at Ben and said, "Why don't you clean your room too? Just in case Kate peeks inside and sees your pile of dirty socks and stacks of books?"

"Who has time to pick up socks?" Ben scoffed. "Chipper and I are in the middle of a super-important project."

"What kind of project?" Willa asked, puzzled. It couldn't be a school project. School had just ended for the summer.

"A top secret, none-of-your-concern project," Ben replied with a mysterious grin. He held up the walkie-talkie he shared with his friend Chipper Starling. Pressing the switch, he spoke into the mouthpiece: "Ben to Chipper. Come in, Chipper. All systems go. Over and out."

"Since when did he get so mysterious?" Dad

chuckled after Ben slipped out of the kitchen.

Willa didn't have time to guess what her brother was up to. She hadn't seen Kate in almost a year and was getting butterflies in her stomach. What Kate thought of Misty Inn and Chincoteague meant a lot to her—so everything had to be perfect.

"Let me know the second Kate gets here," Willa told her parents. "Promise?"

"Promise," Mom and Dad chorused.

Willa grabbed a muffin on her way up the stairs, careful not to drop crumbs. Not that Misty Inn had mice, thanks to New Cat.

As she swung the door open, the WELCOME, KATE sign taped to it fluttered. As she stepped into her room, she was greeted by New Cat himself, lazing on a sleeping bag that Willa would use that week. Kate would sleep in Willa's bed.

"You know I'm crazy about you, New Cat," Willa said, gently nudging the cat off, "but we can't have cat hairs on any beds."

As if he understood, New Cat scurried out of the room. He hadn't left any hairs, but Willa brushed her hand over the sleeping bag just to be sure.

Mom had already made Kate's bed with Willa's pink unicorn-design comforter.

What if Kate thinks unicorns are babyish? Willa worried to herself as she crossed the room. *We are both a year older now.*

But as Willa straightened their favorite friendship picture on her bulletin board, she chased the thought out of her head.

I'm not any different since I left Chicago—so Kate probably isn't either.

Giving her room one last look-over, Willa nodded approvingly. Her room passed her strict inspection. Next up—the ponies.

Willa raced outside to the barn. She had groomed and fed Starbuck and Buttercup early that morning but wanted them to be extra ready for Kate.

From their stalls both ponies seemed happy to see Willa again. Buttercup greeted Willa with a friendly snort. Starbuck nickered softly.

Also there to greet Willa was Amos. The frisky little puppy was Buttercup's best friend and could almost always be found in the barn.

After petting Amos, Willa turned to Starbuck. "We're getting a visitor today," she said, stroking the gentle mare's butterscotch-colored forehead. "And I want you to be on your best behavior for her. Okay, girl?"

Starbuck answered with a puff of breath from her nostrils. To Willa it sounded more like a purr than a snort.

Willa knew Starbuck was special the moment she was delivered to Miller Farm, her grandma Edna's pet sanctuary. Willa and Ben nursed

Starbuck's injured leg until she was well enough to ride—then she walked all the way to the Dunlaps' house, where she knew she belonged.

Now Willa had her own pony, but not just any pony. Starbuck was born on Assateague Island across the bay, world famous for its two herds of wild ponies.

Buttercup let out a confident whinny as if to say, *What about me?* Willa turned to pat Buttercup's velvety muzzle. The chestnut mare with the star between her eyes belonged to her friend Sarah's family, the Starlings. For now Buttercup was an honored guest at Misty Inn, just like Kate would be.

As Willa flicked a piece of hay from Buttercup's mane, she thought again about Kate. Back in Chicago they'd done almost everything together: gymnastics, ice-skating, even horseback-riding lessons.

Willa wished Kate could meet her new friends on Chincoteague Island. But Sarah had just left for wilderness camp on Assateague, where she would learn about the wild ponies there. As for Lena, she cared more about music than horses, so it was piano camp for her.

"Maybe Kate and I will get to ride together," Willa told the ponies excitedly. "How cool would that be?"

Starbuck stomped a hoof on the mud-packed ground. Willa liked to think that meant, *Way cool.*

Stepping back, Willa inspected the barn. Both saddles were oiled and neatly hung on the double saddle rack. The brushes and currycombs were hung too. Everything looked perfect until—

"Oh my gosh," Willa gasped, noticing a green-stained bucket on the ground. "I forgot to scrub out the feed bucket."

She grabbed and turned on the hose. As she began rinsing out the bucket, she thought she heard wheels on the gravelly driveway outside. Willa's heart did a triple flip.

Was it Kate?

Turning off the water and dropping the hose, Willa charged out of the barn. When she saw Kate and her parents, she screamed at the top of her lungs, "You're here!"

Willa ran at jet speed to her friend. As they hugged tightly, Willa wondered if she smelled sweaty from working in the barn. Kate smelled like strawberry shampoo and vanilla shower gel—just as Willa remembered.

"Willa," Kate said after breaking their hug. As she opened her mouth to smile, something silver glinted in the sun. To Willa that could mean only one thing. . . .

"Oh my gosh," Willa gasped. "Kate, you got braces."

Chapter 2

"BRACES WITH COLORED RUBBER BANDS," KATE pointed out. "See?"

"Wow," Willa said, but was a little surprised. Only the older girls back in Chicago wore braces.

"Actually, Ted," Mrs. Worthington told her husband as she examined Kate's smile. "I think Kate's teeth are already straighter."

"It's about time," Kate told Willa. "My cousin Liam once told me I looked like a goofy horse when I laughed."

Willa blinked hard. She didn't know any goofy horses. Gentle, spirited, and friendly horses, but never goofy.

"I can't believe you're really, really here," Willa said, changing the subject. She turned to Kate's parents, Jill and Ted. "Welcome to Chincoteague Island."

Willa spread her arms to hug Kate's parents until she noticed their eyes cast downward. Willa looked down too and gulped. Smeared across the hem of her T-shirt was bright green goop.

"Eww," Kate said, seeing it too. "What's that green slime all over your shirt?"

"It's just fodder," Willa explained. "I was cleaning out the ponies' feed bucket."

"Whatever it is," Kate said, "I'm glad you didn't get it on my brand-new clothes."

Kate struck a little pose to model her outfit to Willa. She was wearing a tunic-style blouse over red capris. On her feet were gold sandals to match her gold earrings.

Nice, Willa thought. *But when did Kate become such a fashionista?*

"Kate told us about your new pony, Willa," Mr. Worthington said. "She read all about Starbuck in your letters."

Willa nodded, happy to talk about Starbuck. "Wait until you meet both ponies, Kate. You won't believe how sweet they are."

"Okay," Kate said with a shrug.

"Ted, Jill, Kate," Dad called. "Welcome to Misty Inn."

Willa turned to see her parents walking over. Both were waving with big smiles.

"Eric, Amelia," Mr. Worthington boomed. "Good to see you."

"After such a long drive, how about a hearty island breakfast?" Mom asked.

"I can whip up some shrimp omelets," Dad offered. "They're one of my specialties at Misty Inn."

"Are we going to eat *again*?" Kate asked her parents. "We just had the most awesome breakfast at the hotel."

"Kate's right," Mrs. Worthington told Mom and Dad. "They had the most incredible buffet in the dining room."

"There were three kinds of egg dishes," Mr. Worthington said, "fresh fruit in season, crunchy granola, Swiss muesli—"

"Don't forget the fro-yo bar," Kate cut in. "With tons of toppings."

Willa glanced at her dad. His smile had become a thin line. He must have felt a little insulted that the Worthingtons didn't want or ask for his breakfast.

"Hey, can't beat a spread like that," Dad said good naturedly. "You know, when I once cooked for a hotel in Chicago, we had a buffet. . . ."

Dad's voice trailed off as Willa watched Kate pull something from her pocket. As she popped off the cap, Willa saw what it was.

"Lip gloss?" Willa asked as Kate spread it over her lips. "You wear lip gloss already?"

"Don't you?" Kate asked. She pressed her lips together, opening them with a loud smack.

"Not really," Willa replied. "I once tried my cousin's, and it felt sticky."

Willa turned to her parents to see how they were doing. The two couples were now laughing together. A good sign.

"We may not have a buffet with Swiss muesli," Mom admitted, "but can I interest you in coffee?"

"We never turn down coffee," Mrs. Worthington said.

"Did I mention the hotel had an espresso bar?" Mr. Worthington asked.

"You didn't, Ted," Dad said. He turned to Willa and Kate. "How about you two? Orange juice? Fresh lemonade?"

"No, thanks, Mr. Dunlap," Kate said politely.

"Let's go to the barn so you can meet the ponies," Willa suggested as the adults headed toward the house.

Kate's lips were now as shiny as her braces. She gave a little shrug and said, "Okay."

When they reached the barn, Kate stopped. "Is it muddy in there? I really don't want to ruin my pedicure."

Pedicure? Willa looked down at Kate's toes. They were polished bright blue. The two big toenails had tiny daisies painted on them.

"There is mud on the ground, but it's very hard packed,"

Willa explained. "Your toes should be fine."

Willa opened the double doors of the barn. Kate practically tiptoed as they walked inside and then immediately held her nose. "What is that stink?" she asked.

Willa started to roll her eyes but thought better of it. "It's just the different smells of the barn; you know, hay and horses, stuff like that."

But Kate wasn't really listening. She looked around, pointed up, and asked, "Is that a hay-loft? Cool."

Willa nodded. "Ben got stuck up there once and had to slide down a rope."

A loud whinny made Kate jump. Willa knew it belonged to Buttercup.

"Meet my friend Sarah's horse, Buttercup," Willa introduced. "Sarah's baby sister fed her buttercups, which made her sick. So she's staying here for now."

Willa gave Buttercup's muzzle a pat before walking over to Starbuck. "And this," she said proudly, "is my pony, Starbuck."

"I still can't believe you have your own horse," Kate said with a smile.

"Neither can I sometimes," Willa admitted. As she stroked Starbuck's forehead, she said softly, "Say hi to Kate, Starbuck."

Starbuck did say hi—with a loud, wet snort.

"Gross," Kate cried, jumping back. "I think he got me. And my antibacterial gel is in my suitcase."

Willa stared at Kate as she shook her hands out. "I thought you were used to horses," she said. "We took riding lessons together in Chicago."

“That was back in second grade,” Kate reminded. “And we both wanted to quit for ice-skating lessons, remember?”

“Right,” Willa said, but she knew it was Kate who’d wanted to switch to skating. Willa loved riding and the horses. But she chose to follow Kate.

“Ice-skating was fun,” Willa admitted. “So was gymnastics. Remember those sparkly orange leotards we wore?”

“I’m still taking gymnastics, Willa,” Kate said, her eyes shining. “I’m even on a team. Which gym do you go to around here?”

“I don’t,” Willa said slowly. “I’m busy with stuff at Misty Inn and taking care of Starbuck.”

“That’s too bad, Willa,” Kate said.

Too bad? Willa didn’t get it. Hadn’t Kate

read her letters or e-mails? The only gymnastics Willa had done since leaving Chicago were a few cartwheels in the Starlings' backyard.

But Willa quickly forgot about gymnastics when she saw Kate stroking Starbuck's soft cheek.

"See how gentle Starbuck is?" Willa asked. "Maybe later we can go on a trail ride together. I'd really like to show you around."

"Maybe," Kate said.

Kate's "maybe" sounded more like a no than a yes to Willa. Wasn't she excited to be on Chincoteague Island?

"Can we go back to the house?" Kate asked. "I could use a glass of orange juice now."

"Sure," Willa said. "I could go for one too."

As they left the barn, Kate asked, "Why is

your parents' bed-and-breakfast called Misty Inn, anyway? Does it have something to do with the weather?"

"No." Willa smiled. "Misty was a pony who swam from Assateague Island to Chincoteague. She's actually a pony in one of my favorite books."

Once inside the house, the girls found their parents in the dining room sipping coffee and chatting over biscotti.

"So how was the barn?" Dad asked.

"Great, Dad," Willa answered. "Kate got to meet Starbuck and Buttercup."

Mrs. Worthington frowned as she stood up from her chair. "No wonder Kate's eyes are so red," she said.

"What do you mean, Jill?" Mom asked.

"Kate suffers from allergies when she's around animals," Mrs. Worthington explained, gently brushing Kate's hair from her eyes.

"Allergic to animals?" Willa asked Kate. "You weren't allergic to animals when I lived in Chicago."

"We never had any pets in Chicago," Kate said.

"There are allergy tablets inside her bathroom kit," Mrs. Worthington explained to Mom and Dad. "Could you make sure Kate takes them?"

"Of course," Dad agreed.

Kate gave a loud sniff then rubbed her eyes.

Oh no, Willa thought with a pang of dread. *What about New Cat? What about Amos? And most of all—what about the ponies?*

Chapter 3

ONCE KATE'S PARENTS LEFT FOR THE ISLAND Harbor Resort and Kate had taken her allergy medicine, Willa said, "We'll have so much fun sleeping in my room. It'll be like having a sleepover every night."

"Just don't forget to sleep," Mom joked.

"You aren't allergic to feathers, too, are you, Kate?" Dad asked.

Willa groaned. "We're not going to have a pillow fight, Dad."

"That's not what I meant," Dad said. "I need a favor over at Mrs. Cornett's house."

"Oh," Willa said. Their neighbor Mrs. Cornett's house was a short hike through the woods. It was also filled with chickens.

"Mrs. Cornett grows vegetables and raises chickens," Willa explained to Kate. "Are you okay with that?"

"Sure," Kate agreed. "My down comforter at home is filled with goose feathers. And I've got a down jacket."

"You should be fine, Kate," Mr. Dunlap said. "Mrs. Cornett is stuck in the house waiting for a delivery. She can't bring by my vegetable order for the day, so I need someone to pick it up now."

Mom looked down at Kate's feet and frowned. "You really ought to put on sneakers before you go. Those sandals aren't ideal for country roads."

"I'll be okay, Mrs. Dunlap," Kate said, wriggling her blue toes.

Willa noticed Ben coming toward the house. He gave Kate a little wave but kept walking.

"Hey, Ben," Willa called. "Come say hello to Kate. You haven't seen her in more than a year."

"No, thanks," Ben called back. "I'll see her later. I'm busy."

When Ben was out of earshot, Willa turned to her parents. "Probably with that top secret project, whatever that is."

"Well, now you have a project too," Dad said with a grin. "Thanks for helping out, girls."

"No problem, Dad," Willa said. She turned to Kate. "Let's go upstairs first. I want to show you my new room. And change into a clean T-shirt."

The friends ran upstairs to Willa's room.

"You'll sleep in my bed, and I'll use my sleeping bag," Willa said, still hoping Kate wouldn't hate the unicorn comforter. "So what do you think of my new room? It's different from the one in Chicago, right?"

"I love this huge mirror," Kate exclaimed, heading straight to Willa's dresser. She leaned over, gazed into the mirror, and squeezed on more lip gloss from a tube.

"Mom found it in an antique store," Willa said slowly. How much lip gloss did Kate need?

Willa changed into a clean T-shirt. Kate put away her lip gloss. A few minutes later they were on their way to Mrs. Cornett's.

"You didn't warn me about goose poop on the ground," Kate complained as they ambled up a rocky path. "Alexa was right. She said Chincoteague would be nothing like Chicago."

"Alexa Santos?" Willa asked. "From our fourth-grade class at school?"

Kate nodded as she flicked a pebble out from between her toes. "Alexa and I are friends now. Well, more than just friends," she explained. "We do practically everything together. She even gave me my first tube of lip gloss."

Willa tried to hide her surprise. Kate had hardly known Alexa when she left Chicago.

Now they were friends. Maybe *best* friends.

"Alexa won first in balance beam at the gymnastics meet," Kate went on. "She even had a girl-boy party for her birthday."

Willa didn't think that was such a big deal. All the parties on Chincoteague so far were for girls and boys. But the way Kate was going on about Alexa, who wasn't even there—that was a huge deal.

Kate stumbled a few more times by the time they reached the cozy yellow cottage. Mrs. Cornett was outside and greeted the girls with a warm smile.

"Guess what?" Mrs. Cornett asked as she led Willa and Kate inside. "My delivery just arrived a few minutes ago. It's in the garden if you'll follow me."

"What were you waiting for, Mrs. Cornett?" Willa asked as they filed out the back door into the garden.

Mrs. Cornett nodded at a cardboard box on the ground. "Why don't you take a peek and see for yourself?"

Willa and Kate hurried over to the box and peered inside.

"Oh my gosh!" Willa gasped.

"Sweet!" Kate exclaimed.

Inside the container were about twenty fuzzy baby ducks.

"These ducklings just arrived Quick Delivery," Mrs. Cornett said. "Or should I say . . . *Quack* Delivery."

Willa and Kate were too busy watching the ducks to laugh at Mrs. Cornett's joke.

"I didn't know you could get baby ducks in the mail," Willa admitted.

"It's perfectly safe if it's done correctly. Some farms and hatcheries deliver overnight, some within two days," Mrs. Cornett explained. "This container has plenty of holes so the ducklings can breathe. There's a soft bedding made out of fine pine shavings too."

"What do they eat?" Kate asked.

"Mostly fine-chopped greens," Mrs. Cornett said, pointing inside the box. "But you'll notice lots of hydrating gel taped along the walls of the container. It's filled with water and nutrients."

Mrs. Cornett introduced the different breeds: Cayuga ducklings, Indian Runner ducks, and Chocolate Runner ducks.

“Chocolate Runner ducks?” Willa giggled. “Do they lay chocolate eggs?”

“No such luck,” Mrs. Cornett said, grinning. “But they will lay some mighty fine white and blue eggs.”

“More eggs?” Willa asked. With all her chickens, and now ducks, Mrs. Cornett had enough eggs to fill the Grand Canyon.

“I know I’ve got a lot of eggs,” Mrs. Cornett said, “but now with Misty Inn using the eggs, it’s a good excuse to grow my brood.”

She pointed to one of the ducklings and added, “That one there’s an Indian Runner. Those ducks are great for mosquito control.”

“I could use one of those,” Kate said as she scratched her arm. “I think I was attacked in the woods by a swarm.”

Willa was about to inspect Kate's bites when one of the babies climbed out of the box. He dropped to the ground and began waddling away.

"Heads up," Mrs. Cornett exclaimed. "We've got a runaway."

"I'll get him, Mrs. Cornett," Willa said, jumping to her feet. "Come on, Kate."

Soon both girls were laughing and running through Mrs. Cornett's garden, zigzagging around plants and flower patches to catch the runaway duck. Kate's sandals didn't even slow her down.

The duckling reached a thick hedge and paused. Willa bent over to gently scoop him up.

"Gotcha," Willa whispered. The tiny duckling felt downy soft and warm in her cupped hands.

"Sooo cute," Kate cooed, stretching out a

finger to pet the fuzzy feathers.

"Once Ben and I had a crazy chicken chase right here in the garden," Willa told Kate. "Ben fell backward onto a raw egg."

"*Eww,*" Kate cried with a laugh.

Willa laughed too. For the first time since Kate had arrived, they were laughing together. Just like they had in Chicago.

Maybe Kate is slowly liking Chincoteague, Willa thought hopefully. *Maybe we will have a blast this week.*

"Mrs. Cornett?" Willa asked. "Can we help you take the ducks out of the container and put them in a crate?"

"I'd love the help," Mrs. Cornett said, "but you girls have some produce to bring back to your dad."

"Oh right." Willa remembered. They were having so much fun in the garden, she forgot about the veggies.

Willa and Kate each picked up a basket and started the walk back to Misty Inn.

"We're having a great time," Willa said excitedly. "Right, Kate?"

Kate answered with a groan. "I didn't know these baskets would be so heavy," she complained, stumbling on the rocky road. "How can

I scratch my mosquito bites while I'm holding this thing? They're so itchy, I want to scream."

Oh well, Willa thought. *I guess maybe just one of us is having a good time.*

"Isn't Ben having dinner with us, Mom?" Willa asked that evening.

It was seven, but the summer sun made it seem as bright as noon. Mom had set up a real Family Farm picnic on the deck just for them.

"Ben is eating at Chipper's house tonight," Mom explained as she poured lemonade into paper cups. "Chipper must miss Sarah while she's away too."

Kate sprayed her arms and legs with a mosquito repellent Mr. Dunlap had given her. As she fanned away the fumes, she asked, "Isn't Sarah your friend, Willa? Why would Ben's friend miss her too?"

Willa explained, "Sarah is Chipper's sister. When we first moved to Chincoteague, I never thought I'd be friends with Sarah, but now we're practically—"

Willa stopped midsentence. She didn't want to say "best friends" and possibly hurt Kate.

"We're practically together all the time," Willa blurted. "Like you and Alexa."

Kate stopped spraying. She picked up her first golden-brown fried oyster and took a bite.

"Mmm," Kate said between chews. "This is totally yummy."

"Better than Chicago pizza?" Willa asked.

"I wouldn't go that far," Kate teased. She

looked around and smiled. “It’s so pretty around here. And it smells a lot better than the city in summer too.”

“Yes.” Willa cheered to herself.

She was having a hard time figuring Kate out today, but she hoped the Chincoteague food and Misty Inn was making its mark, just like it had on Willa.

Chapter 4

"NOOOOOO. MAKE THEM STOP. MAKE IT STOP."

Willa woke with a start. Was she dreaming? Or was somebody—screaming?

"Kate." Willa remembered as she sat up in her sleeping bag.

When she turned to her, Kate's eyes were half closed but her mouth was open in another scream: "Where am I?"

Willa climbed out of her sleeping bag. Something told her that Kate was having a *very* bad dream.

Shaking her friend's leg under the unicorn comforter, Willa whispered, "Kate. Kate, wake up."

"I am up," Kate cried, sitting up. "Why is it so dark in here?"

"Because it's the middle of the night," Willa explained gently. "I think you were having a nightmare."

Kate moaned as she scratched both arms.

"You know what's really a nightmare?" Kate demanded. "These itchy mosquito bites. I feel like armies of ants are marching up my arms."

Willa felt helpless as she watched Kate claw and scratch. Her pink unicorn comforter and what Kate thought of it were the last of her worries now.

Light filled the room as Willa heard the door open. She turned to see Mom standing in the door frame.

"Who just screamed?" Mom asked. She snapped the light on before walking into the room. "Is everything all right?"

"Kate's itchy mosquito bites woke her up," Willa explained. "I think she's afraid of the dark too."

"I am not," Kate hissed.

"Kate, you poor thing." Mom frowned. "I'll be right back with some itch cream that will make you feel better."

Mom left the light on as she hurried for the bathroom cabinet.

“I’m not afraid of the dark, Willa,” Kate insisted. “It’s just that my room in Chicago never gets this dark at night.”

“That’s because we’re in the country,” Willa told her. “In Chicago there’s always a ton of light coming in from the street. Neon signs, car headlights—”

“The light from the top of the Willis Tower,” Kate cut in with a little smile. “It’s so bright, I’ll bet they can see it from space.”

Willa smiled at the mention of the Chicago skyscraper, one of the tallest buildings in the world.

“Remember when we went up to the Skydeck, Kate?” Willa asked. “And when we looked down, the cars looked like teeny, tiny ants—”

"Ants," Kate cried, scratching her arms. "Arrgh. Make it stop. Make it stop."

I had to mention ants, Willa thought glumly.

Mom returned with a tube of cream in one hand, a glass of water in the other.

"And last but not least," Mom said. She dug into the pocket of her robe and pulled out a night-light. "Let there be light."

Willa recognized the yellow night-light shaped like a smiling half-moon. "That's what Ben used to have in his room," she pointed out, "when he was afraid of the dark."

Kate groaned under her breath as she squeezed a squiggle of cream along one arm. "I told you, Willa. I am *not* afraid of the dark."

"I'll plug it in just in case you need to go to

the kitchen for more water," Mom answered. "Nothing wrong with that, right?"

"Thanks, Mrs. Dunlap," Kate agreed.

Mom said good night, snapped off the light, and left the room. As she shut the door, the room darkened except for the soft glow from the man in the moon.

Kate lay back on her pillow, staring up at the ceiling.

"Better?" Willa asked.

"I guess," Kate answered, still gazing up. "But now I can't sleep. I hate it when I can't sleep."

Willa heaved a big sigh. Calming Kate that night was harder than gentling a wild pony.

Pony, Willa thought with a smile. *That's it.*

"Kate?" Willa asked. "How about if I tell you a story?"

Kate wrinkled her nose. "You mean like a princess fairy tale? Aren't we too old for that?"

"This is a story about Starbuck," Willa said, "and how he became my pony."

Still staring up at the ceiling, Kate murmured, "Sure. Go ahead."

Willa sat cross-legged on the bed facing Kate. She took a deep breath and began: "Once upon a time . . . I mean, last fall, Starbuck kept escaping over and over from the field at Miller Farm."

"What's Miller Farm?" Kate asked.

"Remember from my letters? It's the animal rescue center my grandma Edna and grandpa Reed run," Willa explained. "I told you that Grandma Edna is a vet. She takes care of all kinds of animals, even Assateague ponies like Starbuck."

"You mean the ponies that swim to this island?" Kate asked.

"Exactly," Willa replied. "Ben and I thought Starbuck kept escaping because she wanted to go back to Assateague. But late one night when Starbuck escaped again, we followed her deep into the woods."

"The woods?" Kate asked, sitting up in bed. "Where was Starbuck going?"

"Home," Willa replied.

Kate scrunched up her nose. "I thought you said home was Miller Farm. Wasn't Starbuck going the wrong way?"

"That's what we thought," Willa said as she wiggled closer to Kate. "But when we found Starbuck, she was at a spot in the woods almost exactly behind Misty Inn. So Starbuck wasn't trying to leave home—she was trying to go home to us."

Willa waited for Kate's reaction. Why wasn't she saying anything? Did she think the story was babyish? Or boring? But then—

"Wow," Kate blurted. "That was an awesome story, Willa."

"It was?" Willa asked, delighted.

"Totally." Kate nodded. She climbed on top of the comforter and folded her legs facing Willa. "Okay. My turn to tell a story."

"Go for it," Willa urged. She leaned forward and listened closely to Kate's real-life story about the time they went trick-or-treating in Willa's building in Chicago.

"We started with the doorman on the first floor, who gave us chocolate bars," Kate recalled.

"Then we worked our way up to the eighth floor."

Willa pictured her old building. Each floor had five apartments. And eight times five equaled lots of treats.

"Some of my neighbors dressed up and turned their apartments into haunted houses." Willa remembered. "Mr. Wong opened his door dripping with blood."

"It was spaghetti sauce." Kate chuckled. "I could smell the onions and garlic."

Willa loved talking about her building in Chicago. It was a big, old renovated warehouse filled with modern lofts and lots of artists. No wonder their apartments on Halloween resembled horror-movie sets.

"I heard one apartment in that building

really is haunted," Kate said. "The couple who lived there moved out because they heard weird noises at night. And found ghosty-white handprints all over the walls—"

"Too much information," Willa cut in. She hopped off the bed and slid into her sleeping bag. "We'd better go back to sleep. But I really liked your story, Kate."

"And I liked yours," Kate said, trying to stifle a yawn. "But you know what else I like? Reeeeeeally like?"

"No, what?" Willa asked.

"This amazingly cozy unicorn comforter." Kate sighed as she snuggled underneath. "Good night."

Willa smiled. It was a good night and the best way to end the day.

Chapter 5

"FEELING BETTER, KATE?" MOM ASKED THE NEXT morning after Willa and Kate came downstairs.

Dad was busy scrambling eggs with shrimp for the guests' breakfasts. Mom was working on her computer at the kitchen table.

"Thanks, Mrs. Dunlap," Kate answered. "The cream you gave me really helped."

So did our stories, Willa thought happily.

"I just read an e-mail from your mom and dad," Mom told Kate. "They're going on a dolphin-watching tour today. Didn't you want to go too?"

Kate shook her head. "Boats make me seasick," she answered. "And I'd rather spend the day with Willa."

"Great," Willa said. Then quickly added, "Not the seasick part—that you're staying here."

"Why don't you both grab a table in the dining room for breakfast?" Mom suggested.

"Milk and orange juice are already out there," Dad said, facing the stove. "Eggs and sausages coming up."

The Misty Inn guests looked up from their

breakfast plates when the girls walked into the room.

"Good morning," Willa said with a smile.

She and Kate chose a blue table near a sunny window and sat down. As they poured milk into glasses, they could hear the guests chatting to one another.

"Excuse me, but did you hear that blood-curdling scream last night?" one man sitting alone asked the couple at the next table.

The woman's frizzy white hair bounced as she nodded her head. "We sure did, and I'm not surprised. Old Victorian houses like this are famous for being haunted."

"Yeah," Kate whispered to Willa, who was sipping her milk, "so are old Chicago apartment buildings."

Willa lost it. She snorted so hard that milk poured out of her nose. The guests stopped talking to turn and stare.

Quickly wiping her face, Willa whispered, "I think we'd better eat in the kitchen."

"I think you're right," Kate whispered back.

Still giggling, Willa left the dining room with Kate. The day had just begun, and they were already off to a great start.

"This beach is neat, Willa," Kate remarked. "But where's the boardwalk? Where are the resorts?"

Willa wiggled her toes in the sand as they walked along the sugary-white beach. After she and Kate ate breakfast and stopped giggling about the milky mess, they headed straight for the beach.

"Grandpa Reed says that Chincoteague is more interested in wildlife than nightlife," Willa explained. "But there's still tons of stuff to do around here."

"Like what?" Kate asked.

"We've got biking and hiking trails," Willa replied. "We can collect shells or dig for sand crabs."

The look on Kate's face told Willa that crabs weren't an option. That was fine with Willa because what she really wanted to do with Kate was ride the ponies.

Willa knew Kate hadn't been on a horse since their lessons in Chicago. Their lessons had been short and the ponies were always saddled when they arrived. Would Kate feel comfortable riding again? Willa sure hoped so.

"Look," Kate said, picking up a shell. "Maybe I can string this on a cord and wear it as a necklace."

"Kate?" Willa asked slowly. "How would you like to go to Miller Farm and get back up on a horse?"

Kate looked up from the sand, her eyes wide. After giving it a thought, she smiled. "Let's do it," she said.

Willa smiled back.

After a quick lunch of tuna sandwiches and clam chowder at Misty Inn, Willa couldn't get Kate to Grandma Edna's fast enough. Grandma had already agreed over the phone to let Kate ride, so she picked the girls up in her truck and drove them to Miller Farm.

Once in the truck, Willa introduced Kate to her grandmother. The two were meeting for the first time.

"Why aren't we riding Starbuck and Buttercup?" Kate asked Willa.

"The farm has its own horses and riding ring," Willa answered. "Just in case you need a brush-up lesson from Grandma Edna."

"Are there all kinds of animals on the farm," Kate asked, "besides ponies and horses?"

"Goats, chickens, rabbits—yes, all kinds," Willa answered. "You did take your allergy medicine, didn't you?"

"Right after I woke up," Kate confirmed.

When they reached the farm, Grandma Edna turned to Kate. "Willa's told me a lot about you, Miss Kate from Chicago," Grandma

Edna said, raising an eyebrow. "Is it true you once braided a pony's mane when your instructor wasn't looking?"

Kate looked at Willa and said, "You told your grandmother that?"

"It was funny," Willa giggled.

Kate giggled too. "Too bad our instructor didn't think so."

"Okay, you two," Grandma Edna said, "now that you've taken a trip down memory lane, let's take a little trip to the pony field."

Grandma Edna led the way to the fenced-in field where the ponies grazed. When Kate saw the size of Jake, a huge draft horse, her mouth hung open.

"I'm not riding that supersize one," Kate gasped. "Am I?"

"Oh, Jake there is a gentle giant." Grandma Edna chuckled. "But I'm guessing you and Fancy would be the perfect match."

Fancy? Willa's eyes widened at the mention of the tall, shiny bay. "Isn't Fancy a little—"

"High spirited?" Grandma Edna finished. "Just a bit, but only when she's outside the pen."

"Fancy," Kate repeated. "I like her name."

Grandma Edna winked down at Kate's sparkly silver sneakers. "And why am I not surprised?"

Willa led the way to the riding ring, where Fancy grazed. Grandpa Reed had already saddled and haltered the pony for Kate's riding lesson. As the girls and Grandma Edna approached the fence, Fancy lifted her head and pricked her ears.

"How do I know if she likes me?" Kate asked.

"Easy." Grandma Edna reached into the pocket of her vest and pulled out a carrot. "The way to a horse's heart is through her stomach."

Fancy must have seen or smelled the carrot. With a whinny she trotted over to the fence.

"Hold your hand out flat, Kate," Grandma Edna instructed as she handed her the carrot. "This way Fancy will nibble the carrot, not your fingers."

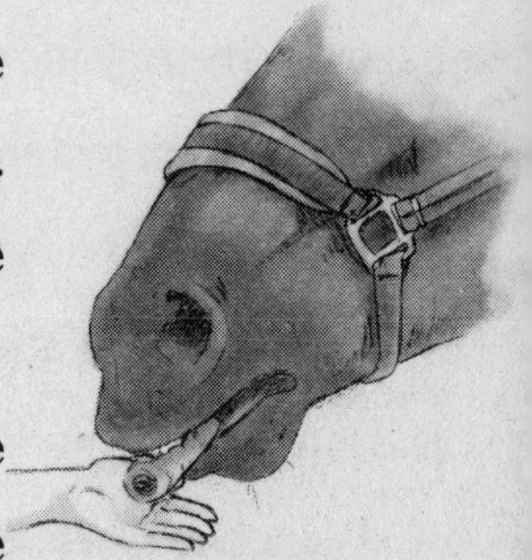

"That tickles," Kate giggled as Fancy ate the carrot out of her hand. She gave a surprised gasp when Fancy nuzzled her shoulder.

Grandpa Reed stood nearby. "Well, will you

look at that?" he said. "The start of a beautiful friendship."

"And the start of your riding lesson," Grandma Edna added. She lifted a helmet hanging from the fence and gave it to Kate. "Ready?"

Kate took a deep breath and said, "Ready."

Grandma Edna walked through the gate into the ring. Kate strapped on the helmet and asked, "Aren't you riding too, Willa?"

"I'd rather watch you ride," Willa admitted. "If that's okay with you."

"It's okay," Kate agreed. She glanced into the ring at Fancy. "Here goes."

Willa took her place outside the fence. She watched as Grandma Edna held two hands under Kate's foot to give her a boost. When Kate was up in the saddle, Grandma Edna stepped way back.

“Now, let’s see what you learned in Chicago,” Grandma Edna called to Kate.

Kate positioned her body in the saddle. She sat straight but not too straight as she firmly held the reins in both hands.

“Remember to relax your shoulders,” Grandma Edna directed. “If you’re tense, Fancy will sense it and might tense up too.”

Willa felt herself tensing up. She so wanted Kate to do a great job and love riding.

So we can ride together again, Willa thought hopefully.

From the middle of the ring, Grandma Edna clicked her tongue. Fancy began to trot. Circling the ring, Kate bounced in the saddle in perfect rhythm with Fancy's moves.

"Go, Kate!" Willa cheered.

After trotting around the ring about half a dozen times, Kate wanted to stop but forgot how.

"Release your leg pressure," Grandma Edna called out. "Now pull in the reins firmly but gently and call, 'Whoa.'"

"Whoa," Kate called, following Grandma Edna's directions. Fancy slowed down, then came to a stop.

"Nailed it," Willa said under her breath. She opened the gate and greeted Kate as she ran over, her eyes shining.

"I did it, Willa," Kate exclaimed.

Willa gave her friend a big hug. She was so proud of Kate for following directions and remembering her lessons.

"Now that you got up close and personal with one of our biggest boarders," Grandma Edna told Kate, "how about meeting the smaller brood at Miller Farm?"

"She means the other rescue animals," Willa explained to Kate. "And there are lots of them."

"Animals, animals, animals," Kate exclaimed. "Does everyone on Chincoteague have tons of pets?"

"Don't you have a pet, Kate?" Grandma Edna asked.

"Only two goldfish," Kate answered as they walked away from the ring. "Their names are Chips and Salsa."

"Allergies," Willa whispered to Grandma Edna. "But it's under control."

To Willa, her first full day with Kate so far was perfect. Things got even better when, after meeting the animals—with no sneezing or itching from Kate—Grandma Edna dropped them off at Four Corners, the yummiest ice-cream parlor in Chincoteague.

When Kate saw the flavor menu, she couldn't believe her eyes. "'Key lime pie,' 'graham cracker,' 'peppermint stick'?" she read out loud. "This place has about as many flavors as Blue Hills."

Willa totally agreed. Blue Hills had been their favorite place for ice cream in Chicago.

"I think I'll have a blackberry bliss cone." Kate narrowed her eyes as she made her decision. "With crushed cookie crumbs on top."

"That flavor has real blackberries in it," Willa pointed out. "Do you like blackberries?"

"Never had any," Kate said. Her finger tapped the glass case as she pointed to the blackberry ice-cream tub. "But I love the purple color, and I don't want anything too gooey to stick to my braces."

"Good point. I'm going to go with peppermint stick." Willa decided. "With rainbow sprinkles."

As they waited for their cones, Willa spotted some kids from school. She proudly introduced Kate to each of them. The others left with their cones, but Willa and Kate carried theirs to a table.

"I can get used to this," Kate said, before pulling a whole blackberry out of her ice cream with her teeth.

"The ice cream?" Willa asked between licks.

Kate gulped down the blackberry and said, "That—and Chincoteague."

Willa stared at Kate over her sprinkled scoop. Did Kate just say what she thought she heard? "You mean you could live here?" she asked. *"Really?"*

"Maybe." Kate nodded. "I'd just need more riding lessons. And tons of Bug Off bug spray."

"Who are you telling to bug off?" someone asked.

Willa looked up. Walking toward their table were Ben and Chipper. Both boys were smiling and carrying ice cream.

"I didn't see you guys come in," Willa said. The boys pulled chairs over to join them.

"That's because we're men of mystery," Chipper answered. "Right, Ben?"

"Check," Ben replied.

"Oh . . . yeah," Willa said. That top secret project they're working on. How could she forget?

"What are you doing today?" Ben asked the girls. "Besides eating ice cream."

Willa described the beach jaunt and Kate's riding lessons. "Kate's having the best time ever," she said. "Right, Kate?"

SNIFF.

Sniff? Willa turned to look at Kate. All of a sudden her face was redder than the cherries in Chipper's ice cream. So was her nose—and it was trembling with each sniff.

"Kate?" Willa asked. "Are you okay?"

"S-s-sure," Kate stammered, her face turning red. "I . . . just . . . have to . . . have to . . ."

Kate threw back her head. Everyone jumped as—*Ah-chooo*—the most earsplitting sneeze Willa had ever heard exploded across the table.

Willa, Ben, and Chipper sat in silence. So did the others in the parlor, staring at Kate. Her supersonic sneeze had blown Chipper's scoop halfway off his cone.

"S-sorry," Kate sniffed. Until her head

rocked back and, "*Ahhh-chooo. Ahhh-chooo. Ahhh-chooooooo . . .*"

Willa's peppermint ice-cream scoop wiggled with each gust. Her rainbow sprinkles had all but blown away. *Yuck.*

When Kate finally stopped, exhausted and

even more red faced, Ben and Chipper stood up.

"Um . . . we've got to go," Chipper murmured.

"Yeah . . . see you later," Ben blurted.

The boys left, tossing their ice creams in the trash can on their way out.

Willa turned to Kate. All she could say was, "Gesundheit."

Kate tossed her soggy cone into a trash can too. She then pulled wads of napkins from the holder to rub her red, raw nose. "I guess I'm allergic to blackberries, too."

"But you said you took your allergy pill this morning," Willa said. "You did, didn't you?"

"I'm supposed to take one every four hours," Kate explained. "I guess I forgot to do that."

Willa frowned. How could Kate forget to take her medicine? But instead of arguing, she took a deep breath and smiled. She never remembered having such a tough time with Kate in Chicago. What had changed?

"Anyone can forget," Willa said. "Why don't we go back to Misty Inn? I'm too full to finish my ice cream anyway."

Kate gave the loudest snort ever. It kind of reminded Willa of the ponies.

"Good," Kate sniffed. "I am *so* over this place."

Willa's heart sank as they left Four Corners. The ice-cream parlor was an epic fail. But didn't Kate just say she could get used to Chincoteague? Walking home, Willa refused to give up.

Willa wanted her best friend to have the same feelings about Chincoteague that she had—and to make this the first of her visits, not the last.

Chapter 6

"KATE, HONEY, I FEEL AWFUL," MOM SAID, AFTER she saw Kate's sneeze-ravaged face. "I should have reminded you to take your next pill."

"Maybe you'd better take it easy the rest of the day, Kate," Dad suggested.

"We can watch a movie over a huge bowl of Dunlap family-favorite popcorn," Willa exclaimed. "Kate, you used to love my dad's popcorn back in Chicago, remember?"

"That was before I had braces, Willa." Kate sighed. "Popcorn gets stuck between the metal and the rubber bands."

"I didn't know," Willa said.

"Alexa has braces too, so she gets it," Kate said. "She also has allergies."

"Oh," Willa said, then bit her lip to keep from screaming. Or crying.

"You can still watch a movie or play a game," Mom suggested. "Why don't you borrow my tablet and take it upstairs?"

"Thanks, Mom," Willa said. She turned to Kate and added, "I know a great site with free movies. You can pick what we watch since you're the guest."

Upstairs, Willa and Kate sat side by side on

the floor, leaning against the bed. Just like they used to do in Willa's room in Chicago.

Willa was just about to search for the site when—

"Wait," Kate said. "Can I Skype Alexa first?"

Willa's hands froze on the keypad. "Do you have to? *We* were going to watch a movie."

"We will—after we say hi to Alexa," Kate said. "This way you can see how cool she really is."

Willa didn't know what to do or say. So when Ben and Chipper burst into the room, she was almost relieved.

Both boys looked like they were playing dress-up. Ben wore a red bandanna around his head and a pirate's eye patch. On Chipper's head was a sea captain's hat and in his mouth—a corncob pipe.

"What are you doing?" Willa asked.

Chipper pointed to Kate, then with a deep voice shouted, "Thar she bloooowwwws. Thar she blooowwwws."

"See the spout, me hearties," Ben bellowed. "See the spout."

"What are they talking about?" Kate asked Willa.

"Um . . . they're pretending you're a whale," Willa explained. "I think."

Kate glared at the boys. "Did you just call me a whale?"

"Just your sneeze." Chipper chuckled. "It's like a whale spouting water from his blowhole."

"A whale of a sneeze." Ben guffawed.

"That is not funny," Kate snapped at the boys. "Go away."

"Yes, please," Willa agreed. "Go back to your silly top secret project."

"Wait till you see what we're working on," Ben said.

"You'll feel pretty silly for thinking it was silly."

The boys traded a fist bump, then darted out of the room.

"Boy, Ben has really changed since moving here. He used to be *so* quiet. I don't know which way I like him better," Kate said. Then she sighed and added, "It's so good to be an only child. What do you think their secret project is?"

"Who knows?" Willa admitted. "Ben and Chipper are always talking about staging a frog race. Maybe they're training some super frog somewhere."

"They race frogs around here?" Kate wrinkled her nose. "That is so disgusting."

Willa didn't think frogs were disgusting—especially after seeing so many of all sizes and colors on Chincoteague Island. There were bullfrogs, southern leopard frogs, green tree frogs—all kinds.

"Frog races did happen on Chincoteague," Willa admitted, "but I've never seen one."

"Good," Kate said. "Now what movie should we watch?"

Willa made sure not to remind Kate about Alexa. She was about to turn back to the tablet when she remembered something important.

"I need our password for the movie site," Willa said. "I'll go downstairs and get it from my dad."

Leaving Kate in the room, Willa bounded down the stairs. She was glad Kate had changed her mind about Alexa.

Downstairs, Willa scribbled the password on a notepad. She tore off the page, thanked Dad, then ran back upstairs.

"Got it," Willa said, stepping into her room. "Now we can—"

Willa stopped midsentence when she saw Kate holding a shiny pink phone.

"You have a phone, too?" Willa asked, surprised. "Since when?"

"My parents gave it to me for emergencies," Kate said, slipping the phone into her pocket. "Can we pick out a movie now?"

Kate didn't seem to be having an emergency, so Willa smiled and said, "One blockbuster coming up."

Kate picked out a movie about a family who adopts a talking dog. Except for the talking part, the dog reminded Willa of Amos.

When they were done watching the movie, Kate unpacked a bottle of purple nail polish and painted Willa's toenails. At first Willa wasn't sure if she liked it, but when the girls compared toenails, she couldn't help but smile.

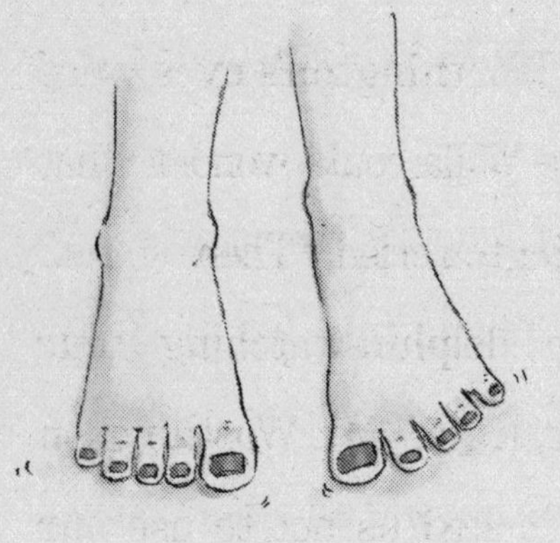

"Your first pedicure," Kate declared when she was finished, and Willa wiggled her toes. "What do you think?"

"I like it. I really do," Willa said. "Let's go downstairs and show Mom."

Giggling, Willa and Kate raced down the stairs—almost bumping into the woman with white frizzy hair on her way up.

"Sorry," Willa called back.

When they reached the bottom of the stairs, Willa saw her mom and dad standing in the parlor. Also there were Mr. and Mrs. Worthington.

"Hi, Mom, Dad," Kate said, surprised.

Both Mr. and Mrs. Worthington's eyes were wide with worry. Before Willa could wonder what was wrong, Mrs. Worthington cried, "There she is."

"We were on the dolphin-watching tour when we saw your text, Kate," Mr. Worthington explained. "Our guide asked us not to use our phones until the boat ride was over."

What text? Willa wondered, until she remembered seeing Kate with her phone.

"You scared us to death when you described your allergies," Mrs. Worthington told Kate. "Honey, are you all right?"

So that's what the emergency was, Willa thought.

But why hadn't Kate told her that she texted her parents about her allergy? Didn't she and Kate once tell each other everything?

Chapter 7

"I'M OKAY NOW, MOM. DID YOU SEE A LOT OF dolphins from that boat?" Kate said, trying to change the subject.

"About two or three," Mr. Worthington said, still studying Kate. "You said you were attacked by mosquitoes, too."

That makes two emergencies, Willa thought sadly.

"I was bitten up, Dad," Kate agreed. "But Mrs. Dunlap gave me this awesome cream."

"I should have made sure she took her allergy medication too," Mom admitted. "I'm sorry, Jill."

"No apology necessary," Mr. Worthington said. "That's *our* job."

"From now on we'll send Kate a series of reminder texts," Mrs. Worthington said, "whether we're on a boat or not."

Willa gazed over at Kate, who didn't look all that thrilled with her mother's suggestion.

"I have a plan too," Mr. Dunlap said with a grin. "How about if we all have dinner tonight, here at Misty Inn?"

"Dinner?" Mrs. Worthington asked.

"Here?" Mr. Worthington blurted.

"You bet," Dad remarked. "I've got a steaming seafood casserole in the oven for a crowd."

"And there's Caesar salad on the menu," Mom added.

Willa felt her mouth water. Dad's seafood casserole was the best. So were his salads.

"Actually, we were planning on having dinner at that new seafood place they opened on the mainland," Mr. Worthington explained. "It's called Clams."

"James Willard, the head chef, is from Chicago," Mrs. Worthington added. "His wedge salad with blue cheese is supposed to be succulent."

"So . . . you want to go there instead?" Dad asked.

"How can we not?" Mr. Worthington asked.

"Who would expect to find a celebrity chef around here?"

Ouch. Willa frowned. Her dad may not have been a celebrity chef—but he was incredibly talented. Everyone in Chincoteague thought so.

"Then Clams it is," Dad said, being a good sport. "I kind of wanted to try it myself. Check out the competition."

"Me too," Mom said, although Willa didn't actually believe her. We can ask Mrs. Cornett to hold the fort while we're gone.

"Super," Ted declared. "Our treat."

"Oh, no, no," Mom insisted. "We'll go dutch."

"Dutch? I thought we were having seafood," Mr. Worthington joked. "But, seriously, we insist."

Willa looked at her parents for their answer. They each smiled and chorused, "Thanks."

"Fab," Kate cheered. "We're going to a fancy restaurant just like in Chicago."

Willa was sure her dad's cooking was just as good—even better than that celebrity chef's. And who was James Willard, anyway? He didn't even have his own cooking show.

Kate's parents returned to their hotel to freshen up. They would drive to Clams and meet Kate and the Dunlaps there later.

The girls ran upstairs to change. Willa put on a sundress and yellow flats. Kate wore skinny white jeans and a nautical-style top. On her feet this time were silver sandals decorated with sparkly gems.

"Why didn't you wear sandals, Willa?" Kate

asked as they all climbed into the car. "Nobody will see your pedicure."

"That's okay," Willa said as she reached for her seat belt. "I'll wear flip-flops tomorrow."

On the ride to the mainland, Willa sat between Kate and Ben in the backseat. At first, everyone was quiet. But then Willa glanced over at Kate, who was spreading on more lip gloss.

"It smells like strawberry," Willa pointed out.

"Strawberry kiwi," Kate explained. "Want to try some?"

"No, thanks," Willa replied.

"Oh, right, you don't like lip gloss," Kate said. "What do you use when you get chapped lips?"

Ben leaned over to say, "Grandma Edna gave us this cream she uses on cow udders when they get dry."

"Ben!" Willa said. But it was too late.

"Are you serious?" Kate cried. "You use cow cream on your lips?"

Willa shrugged. "It works. It makes my lips really smooth."

"You mean *s-mooooooo-th,*" Ben teased, and both girls couldn't help but laugh.

"So what do you think of this place, kids?" Mr. Worthington asked when they were all seated at a big square table.

Willa looked around the dining room bathed in lavender light. Most seafood places they visited had red-and-white-checkered tablecloths and fishnets hanging from the ceiling. Clams had black lacquered tables and white tufted chairs—shaped like clams, of course. To

Willa there was nothing about Clams that said fish except the smell from the kitchen.

"It's . . . very modern," Willa said politely.

"Where are the fish kites?" Ben asked. "Our favorite seafood restaurant in Chincoteague has fish kites on the ceiling—"

"It's lovely, Ted," Mom cut in.

Willa couldn't find popcorn shrimp on the menu, so she and Ben ordered fish tacos. Kate chose linguini with scallops.

After a waitress named Delilah took their orders, the adults spoke among themselves, mostly about Chicago. Willa glanced at Ben sculpting his linen napkin into a sailboat.

"How's your top secret project going?" Willa asked him.

"And what is it, anyway?" Kate wanted to know.

"It's coming along great," Ben answered. "And if I told you what it is, it wouldn't be top secret."

When their orders arrived, everyone seemed happy with their dishes. Everyone except Kate's father.

"My pistachio-crusted cod is a bit overcooked." Mr. Worthington sighed. "So much for Chef Willard."

Mrs. Worthington dabbed the corner of her lips with her napkin. "Why don't you tell us what you did today, girls," she asked, "besides that disastrous trip to the ice-cream parlor?"

Kate's mouth was full, so Willa answered for her: "Kate rode a horse at Miller Farm. Her name is Fancy."

"Kate also looked sharp in her riding boots and blazer when she took lessons," Mrs.

Worthington recalled. "Too bad there was always that horsey smell."

Willa glanced up from the roll she was buttering. Kate's mom said "horsey smell" like it was a bad thing.

"Do you think you'll ever want to take riding lessons again, Kate?" Mrs. Dunlap asked.

"I certainly hope not," Mrs. Worthington piped in. "The drive from our building to the barn was ridiculously long."

"And Kate doesn't need riding lessons," Mr. Worthington remarked. "She's busy taking gymnastics."

Willa's stomach was in knots. Was it because of the tacos? Or because it seemed like the Dunlaps and Worthingtons were as different as night and day?

"You and Willa used to carpool together to gymnastics." Dad remembered. "The two of you laughed so hard, the car would shake."

"I take gymnastics with Alexa now," Kate said, her eyes shining. "We're going to be on the same gymnastics squad this fall and take dance and theater together."

Willa's stomach twisted at the mention of Alexa. Was she jealous?

I made new friends in Chincoteague, Willa told herself. *Why shouldn't Kate make new friends too?*

"Do you miss taking gymnastics, Willa?" Mrs. Worthington asked, interrupting her thoughts. "You probably would have gone to the next level like Kate."

"I did like gymnastics," Willa replied. "But taking care of my Starbuck keeps me busy."

"I almost feel like Fancy is my pony now," Kate declared. "We're definitely going riding tomorrow, right, Willa?"

"Right," Willa agreed. She was glad Kate

wanted to go riding again. But something about the way she insisted made Willa a little uncomfortable. She just wished she could relax. When did being friends become such hard work?

After dessert everyone was stuffed. Mom and Dad chuckled politely when Mr. Worthington joked he was stuffed to the "gills."

On their drive home Ben fell fast asleep. Willa and Kate were sleepy too as they gazed out the back window.

"I never see so many stars in Chicago," Kate whispered.

"Mmm-hmm," Willa agreed.

"And we are going riding tomorrow," Kate whispered, careful not to wake Ben up. "This time on the beach."

"Okay," Willa agreed. "I can ask Grandma Edna to ride with us—"

"No. Just you and me," Kate insisted. "And I want to ride Fancy."

Fancy? Willa knew Grandma Edna wouldn't let them take one of her horses out without her supervision. Besides, Fancy was too high spirited to ride outside the ring, especially for a beginner like Kate. She needed a calm, gentle pony.

There's only one horse I trust with Kate, Willa thought to herself, *and that's Starbuck.*

But she wasn't convinced that was such a great idea either.

Chapter 8

"WHY CAN'T I RIDE FANCY?" KATE ARGUED THE next morning. "You saw how great she was with me in the ring yesterday."

"That's just it," Willa tried to explain for what seemed like the hundredth time. "Fancy is calm in the ring, but outside she can be skittish."

Kate heaved a big sigh before saying, "Okay. I'll ride Starbuck."

Willa heaved a sigh too—of relief. "Thanks."

But convincing Kate to ride Starbuck was just the first part of the job. Willa had written a new list early that morning while Kate was still asleep:

BEFORE THE BEACH

1. Call Mr. Starling for permission to ride Buttercup.

2. Get permission from Mom and Dad.

3. Tack the ponies.

"Mr. Starling is Sarah and Chipper's father," Willa said as they walked downstairs. "He's also a saltwater cowboy."

When Willa saw Kate's puzzled expression,

she explained, "His job is to round up wild ponies on Assateague Island."

"Wild ponies like Starbuck?" Kate asked.

Willa nodded. "Once Buttercup is ready, he'll use her for the pony swim."

Before phoning Mr. Starling, Willa ate a big breakfast. Kate was still eating her blueberry yogurt when Willa made the call. . . .

"So you want to ride Buttercup on the beach," Mr. Starling said, after hearing Willa's plan.

"Yes, Mr. Starling," Willa said. "I know I've only ridden Buttercup a few times, when Sarah and I swapped, but there were never any problems."

Willa gripped the phone waiting for Mr. Starling's response. Finally he said, "You have my okay. I've seen you ride with Sarah, and you have great instincts with horses."

"Thanks, Mr. Starling," Willa said, giving Kate a thumbs-up sign. Kate returned it with a spoons-up sign.

"And Buttercup is gentle," Mr. Starling went on. "She's also very reliable."

Almost as reliable as Starbuck, Willa thought, *who is the sweetest, most loyal pony I know.*

After ending the call, Willa said, "We're almost there, Kate. Next step is to get permission from Mom and Dad."

"So much permission!" Kate exclaimed. "Are we riding horses or a space shuttle?"

Willa might as well have asked for a trip to space, because her parents were the toughest sell. . . .

"I'm not sure you should ride on the beach

by yourselves," Mom admitted. "It's been a while since Kate took riding lessons—"

"Kate did great at Grandma's farm, Mom," Willa cut in. "Plus, she'll be riding Starbuck, who's super gentle."

"Both ponies are gentle and trusting," Dad told Mom. "As long as Willa and Kate walk—not race—the ponies on the beach, it shouldn't be a problem."

Mom tapped a thoughtful finger on the counter. "Okay," she finally said. "But no trotting or galloping whatsoever."

"Deal," Willa agreed.

"Double deal," Kate added.

"Just as important, Kate," Mom said, "did you take your allergy pill? You'll be around ponies most of the day."

Kate nodded. "I took one at breakfast, Mrs. Dunlap."

"Well, okay, then. I'll make you sandwiches to take to the beach," Dad offered. "I can cut up carrots for the ponies too."

"Thanks, Dad. Thanks, Mom," Willa said. With just two days left to Kate's visit, she was certain today was going to be Kate's favorite yet.

Willa packed the lunches and carrots in a small backpack. She swung it from her hand as she and Willa headed for the barn. On their way they passed Ben pulling a wagon filled with lumber and coils of rope.

"What's that for?" Willa asked him.

Ben looked over his shoulder as he kept walking. "Still not ready to tell. But come over to the Starlings later and check it out."

"Why is he being so secretive? It's probably no big deal," Kate said.

"Wood . . . rope," Willa thought out loud. Her eyes suddenly lit up. "Maybe a tree house—with a rope ladder. What do you think?"

"I guess," Kate said. "Can we walk faster? I really want to start riding."

Puzzled, Willa glanced at Kate. Why was she so anxious to ride on the beach? And why was she in a hurry all of a sudden? Willa thought of asking Kate but didn't want to spoil her excitement.

"I want to ride too," Willa agreed, picking up her pace. "But before we do, we have to tack the horses. Do you remember what that is?"

"Sure, I do," Kate answered. "Tack is the equipment horses wear for riding. Our instructor in Chicago gave us a demonstration once."

Amos seemed to be expecting the girls as he stood in front of the barn. He yipped loudly as Willa opened the barn doors. She was pleased that Kate didn't mention the barn's smell this time.

With Amos at her heels, Willa walked to Starbuck's and Buttercup's stalls. Both ponies seemed at ease, their eyes soft, their mouths relaxed.

"Let's start with the saddles," Willa suggested. "Since you'll be riding Starbuck, we'll saddle her first."

The two friends worked as a team. Willa secured Starbuck to the barn's hitching post. Kate laid a soft saddle pad over her back.

"Saddles are heavy," Willa said, pointing to

the double saddle rack. "Do you want me to help you take it down?"

"No, thanks." Kate flexed a muscle in one arm. "I take gymnastics, remember?"

Kate lifted Starbuck's saddle from the rack. Willa watched as Kate carefully saddled the pony. But when it came time to tighten the girth, Starbuck protested with a grunt.

"You're tying it too tight," Willa pointed out. She stepped in to loosen the buckle. Starbuck thanked Willa with a sigh.

"What's next?" Kate asked.

"Why don't you get Starbuck's bridle?" Willa suggested. "It's on the row of hooks, the one closest to the door."

While Kate went for the bridle, Willa whispered softly into Starbuck's ear, "I know you'll take very good care of my friend, won't you, girl?"

Starbuck rested her cheek lightly against Willa's. That told Willa she had nothing to worry about.

"Good girl," Willa told her pony.

Kate did much better with the bridle than the girth. She joked about the bit, the piece that went inside the horse's mouth.

"It reminds me of my braces," Kate giggled.

Willa took care of Buttercup next. After both ponies were tacked, the friends walked them out of the barn. Willa watched as Kate successfully mounted Starbuck without a boost.

"I am so ready," Kate called down from the saddle. "Come on, Willa. Let's ride."

"Wait," Willa said as she pulled herself up on Buttercup. "Don't forget that Starbuck is super sensitive. She has a soft mouth so go easy on the reins. And no trotting." Willa pointed to Starbuck's side and added, "Starbuck doesn't take much leg, either. You only need to squeeze lightly."

"Got it," Kate said.

Since Buttercup wasn't her own horse, Willa was extra careful. She slackened the reins, squeezed her calves gently against Buttercup's sides, then clucked her tongue. Buttercup moved forward.

Kate did the same with Starbuck. Soon both ponies and their riders were calmly walking away from the barn.

"See you later, Amos," Willa called back.

Willa took the lead. The plan was to walk along a few roads until they got to a path that would take them straight to the beach.

"Where are the cars, Willa?" Kate called.

"It's the middle of the week," Willa called back. "Most of the heavy traffic on Chincoteague is on weekends."

A few cars slowed down as they passed the girls, careful not to startle the horses.

Willa smiled to herself as she listened to the soft hoofbeats. Kate was doing a good job riding Starbuck. And Starbuck was doing a good job caring for Kate—as promised.

When the girls reached the beach, they were greeted by the sound of rustling waves. Only a few beach towels dotted the sand since it was still early in the day.

Willa tugged on Buttercup's reins until she came to a stop. Kate did the same, stopping Starbuck. The two ponies stood side by side facing the water. This was a dream come true for Willa, and she hoped Kate felt the same way.

Willa gazed out at Assateague Island across the bay, its tall, wild grasses swaying in the summer breeze. Sarah was there now learning all about the wild ponies. But for the first time that week, Willa didn't miss Sarah as much.

"Look, Kate, there's Assateague," Willa pointed out. "Where Starbuck was born."

"Cool," Kate said.

But when Willa looked at Kate, she wasn't looking at Assateague or the bay. She was too busy steering Starbuck *around* Buttercup.

"Kate, what are you doing?" Willa asked.

Kate didn't answer. Instead, she thumped Starbuck's side with a hard kick. Starbuck gave a startled neigh. She then lifted her tail—and took off.

Chapter 9

WILLA SAT FROZEN IN HER SADDLE AS KATE galloped Starbuck down the beach. Hadn't they made a deal with Mom and Dad not to gallop the ponies? What was Kate thinking?

"Kate!" Willa shouted as she steered Buttercup in Starbuck's direction. "Slow down. Slow Starbuck down."

Kate didn't pull back on the reins. Her hold

on the reins was loose. Too loose. And the way she bounced in the saddle was totally out of sync with Starbuck's rhythms.

A sick feeling came over Willa—a feeling that something bad was about to happen. And suddenly . . .

Kate screamed, toppled out of the saddle, the rein still in her hand. As she fell, she gave Starbuck's mouth a sharp jerk.

"Oh nooo!" Willa cried. A sand dune softened Kate's fall, but she could see the whites of Starbuck's frightened eyes as she reared up and groaned.

Willa had to help Starbuck. Not wanting to startle Buttercup by galloping, she jumped out of the saddle. Then with Buttercup in tow, Willa hurried down the beach to her pony in distress.

Kate was still clutching the rein when Willa reached them. Grabbing the rein, Willa loosened the slack. Starbuck's ears flicked back and forth before letting out a deep breath.

"Easy, easy," Willa softly repeated. When she was sure Starbuck was calm, she inspected her mouth. Running her hand along Starbuck's lips, Willa was relieved not to find any cuts or scrapes.

"I don't know how it happened, Willa," Kate finally said from her spot in the sand. "Starbuck just took off like a jet."

"After you kicked her hard," Willa said pointedly. "We *promised* my parents we'd walk the ponies on the beach. Why did you gallop Starbuck?"

Kate was silent, but she gave Willa a small smile.

Willa wasn't smiling. With Buttercup's and Starbuck's reins in one hand, she reached down to Kate with her other. "Here. Let me help you up."

"With horse spit all over your hand?" Kate refused. "No, thanks."

"Horse spit?" Willa asked.

"Your hand was in Starbuck's mouth," Kate explained as she pulled herself up from the sand. "And see? I'm fine."

"You could be hurt and not know it," Willa said. "If you have your phone, we can call Mom and Dad."

"I'm fine," Kate repeated. "Let's just ride the ponies back to the barn."

Willa shook her head. After what just happened, Starbuck could still be jumpy.

"No, Kate. We're going to walk the ponies home," Willa told Kate. "I mean, I'll walk them."

Kate nodded as if to say fine. "I am so over horseback riding anyway. No wonder I switched to gymnastics."

Kate walked sulkily ahead of Willa and the ponies. By now Willa's head was spinning with all kinds of feelings. Did she push Kate to like horseback riding when she wasn't ready? Then again, it was Kate who took advantage of Starbuck's trusting nature.

And by doing that, Willa thought sadly, *she took advantage of me.*

The walk along the road was awkward and quiet. Until Kate turned to say, "I thought you were going to wear flip-flops today instead of sneakers. To show off your pedicure."

Willa stared at Kate. Flip-flops for horseback riding? Was she serious?

"It's a good thing I didn't wear flip-flops today," Willa declared. "I wouldn't have been able to run and help Starbuck."

Kate stared back at Willa. She faced forward to hide her hurt and continued walking.

As they continued farther up the road, the girls passed the Starling house. Willa could see Mr. Starling busily working in the garden.

"Well, hi there," Mr. Starling called. "How was your ride on the beach?"

Willa didn't want to tell Mr. Starling what really happened. She was pretty sure Kate didn't either.

“It was great, Mr. Starling,” Willa called back, forcing a smile. “Buttercup was a sweetie as usual.”

“That’s what I thought,” Mr. Starling remarked.

The Starlings’ front door swung open. Ben and Chipper stepped outside sipping bottles of lemonade through straws.

“Inventing is thirsty work,” Chipper declared.

“I’ll bet even Thomas Edison needed lemonade breaks,” Ben said after a long slurp.

“Inventing?” Willa asked, scrunching her brow. “What are you guys inventing?”

“It’s called the Starling/Dunlap Zipster,” Chipper announced proudly.

“Dunlap/Starling,” Ben told Chipper. “You promised.”

“The what?” Willa asked.

"Only the most amazingly awesome obstacle course in the world," Chipper explained, "with its own zip line."

Willa smiled. So that's what Ben's rope and lumber was for. It sounded awesome.

She wondered if it really would work.

"Come on, Willa, Kate," Ben called. "Try out the Zipster. You won't be sorry."

"Unless it isn't safe," Kate murmured.

Mr. Starling smiled at the girls. "I helped out and rode it myself. It's safe and pretty amazingly awesome, like Chipper said."

Willa was curious, but Starbuck's whiskers tickled her arm as if to say, *Remember us?*

"We want to get the ponies back to the barn first," Willa said. "Maybe we'll check it out later. Right, Kate?"

"Maybe," Kate said, her eyes cast downward.

Why is Kate the sad one? Willa wondered. She was still kind of angry at Kate for totally disobeying her parents and doing whatever *she* wanted. Starbuck—and Kate—could have been badly hurt.

The girls continued on their way home, Willa still holding both reins. Riding the Zipster sounded like fun. But after their terrible morning on the beach, Willa felt their friendship would never recover.

Why did I ever agree to ride the ponies on the beach? Willa thought sadly. *What was I thinking?*

Chapter 10

BY THE TIME WILLA GOT BOTH PONIES BACK TO the barn, she was exhausted. There was work to do, unsaddling and sponging them off, which she did all alone. Kate had gone straight to the house.

Willa wondered if Kate was mad at her for being mad when she galloped Starbuck? That thought made Willa even more annoyed at Kate.

Her chores done, Willa sat in the backyard

under a tree, where she had dropped her backpack. The last thing she wanted to do was go inside the house. How could she tell her parents what had happened? How could she admit to her mom that she was right to be worried?

Shutting her weary eyes, Willa leaned against the tree. She could feel herself drifting off to sleep when—

"Hi."

It was Kate.

Willa's eyes popped open. She turned to see Kate standing few feet away. With a sigh, Kate plopped down next to Willa. She opened a tube of lip gloss and squeezed it all over her lips.

"Coconut pineapple," Kate explained. "But for some reason I taste banana."

This time Willa gagged at the gross smell. Lip gloss, lip gloss, lip gloss.

"Why do you keep doing that?" Willa demanded. "To look older? More glam? Because Alexa does it?"

"None of that," Kate answered. "There's something about my braces that makes my lips dry. They get crazy chapped, even in the summer. It is so painful and annoying."

"Oh," Willa said. She had no idea Kate's braces made her lips dry. No wonder she needed so much lip gloss.

"And don't worry about telling your parents what happened on the beach," Kate said, "because I already told them."

"You did?" Willa turned to stare at Kate. "What did you tell them?"

"The truth," Kate said. "I told them it was my fault for galloping Starbuck on the beach. And it wouldn't happen again."

"Thanks." Willa smiled. She hadn't expected Kate to take responsibility but was glad she did.

"I really am sorry, Willa," Kate admitted. "I was just showing off on Starbuck, to prove that I could ride too."

"You don't have to show off to me," Willa insisted. "We're friends."

Kate plucked a piece of grass, twirling it between her fingers. "I know we are, but ever since I got here, I saw how much you've changed since you left Chicago."

"*I've* changed?" Willa asked, surprised. "Me? In what way?"

"You're amazing with horses and riding,"

Kate explained. "You're an expert on Chincoteague and Assateague. You even like doing your disgusting chores."

Willa couldn't believe her ears. She thought *Kate* had changed since Chicago. All this time Kate was thinking the same about her.

"You're different too," Willa admitted. "You're so into clothes all of a sudden. Everything you wear matches and is so . . . trendy."

"Thanks." Kate smiled. "I did start liking clothes this year. I think I might want to be a fashion designer when I grow up."

"You do?" Willa asked, surprised at Kate's plans.

"What do you want to be?" Kate asked.

"Maybe a vet," Willa replied. "Like my grandma Edna."

"You'd make an awesome vet," Kate remarked.

"And you'd make an awesome fashion designer," Willa declared with a smile.

The friends high-fived. And in that instant, any differences between them seemed to disappear. They caught up on everything they missed from each other's lives: Kate had won third prize at the school art fair. Willa had helped her grandma Edna deliver a baby colt. Kate had gone to her first Chicago Cubs game, and Willa had learned to kayak. As they talked, Willa pulled out the sandwiches her dad had packed for the beach, for a picnic-style lunch. They were so busy chatting and chewing that Willa didn't notice Dad strolling over from the house.

"Good news, girls," Dad called. "One of our

guests needs to leave early so guess who's agreed to check in?"

"My parents?" Kate guessed with a smile.

Dad nodded. "For the last two nights of your vacation."

"Kate, that is so cool," Willa exclaimed. "Now everybody will be together."

"It is cool," Kate agreed. "But if it's okay with you, I'd still like to stay in your room."

"Of course it's okay," Willa said.

As Dad headed back to the house, Kate asked, "What should we do now? Ride that Zipster your brother invented?"

"For sure." Willa nodded. "But there's something else I'd rather do first."

"More horseback riding?" Kate asked carefully.

"Nope," Willa said as they both stood up.

"I want you to show me everything you and Alexa learned in gymnastics."

"You do?" Kate asked, surprised.

Willa nodded. "We'll go to the pasture where the grass is nice and soft. After that we'll try the Zipster—but only if we are one hundred percent sure it's safe."

"Hey, I've already taken one giant fall today," Kate joked.

"And if you fall again," Willa said with a smile, "I'll be right there to lend a hand . . . without horse spit."

As they raced each other to the pasture, Willa knew she and Kate would always be friends. No matter what. She also knew they would always have the most awesome memories. And now, they had two more days to make more.

ACKNOWLEDGMENTS

Thanks to the entire Aladdin team for bringing this book to life. Karen Nagel's enthusiasm and humor make any project a pleasure. Thanks to her and to Fiona Simpson for trusting this life-long city girl to imagine life on Chincoteague Island. Much thanks to Kristin Earhart for her wonderful vision of Misty Inn and its characters. Her knowledge and love of horses were incredibly helpful and inspiring. Thanks also to Serena Geddes, whose illustrations bring so much sparkle to the series, and to Laura Lyn DiSiena, for beautifully designing the book. Last but not least, a huge thanks to my family and forever friends—you're always there to lend support and an occasional ear for my ideas, day or night.